Max and Maggie in
SPRING

Written by Janet Craig
Illustrated by Paul Meisel

Troll Associates

For Damon in spring—
J.C.

Library of Congress Cataloging-in-Publication Data

Palazzo-Craig, Janet.
Max and Maggie in spring / written by Janet Craig;
illustrated by Paul Meisel.
p.   cm.—(Nice mice)
Summary: Two mice friends clean house and enjoy beautiful
spring flowers.
ISBN 0-8167-3350-3 (library) — ISBN 0-8167-3351-1 (pbk.)
[1. Spring—Fiction. 2. Mice—Fiction.
3. Friendship—Fiction.]   I. Meisel, Paul, ill. II. Title.
III. Series: Palazzo-Craig, Janet.   Nice mice.
PZ7.P1762Maws 1995
[E]—dc20   94-39037

10   9   8   7   6   5   4   3   2   1

CONTENTS

SPRING FEVER

Maggie awoke one fine spring morning. She felt the warm sunshine. She breathed the fresh spring air. Then she closed her eyes.

"What a beautiful day," said Maggie. "I believe it is the perfect day for doing nothing at all!"

Maggie happily fell back to sleep. She did not know that someone was on his way to her house at that very moment. That someone was her good friend, Max.

Max whistled a happy tune. His small feet carried him lightly along.

"What a fine day," said Max. "It's a perfect day for spring cleaning. I'll go and help Maggie. She'll be so happy!"

Max ran up the stairs and opened Maggie's door. "Maggie," he called, "it's me! Let's get to work!"

Maggie sat up in bed and stared at her friend.

"Spring has sprung!" said Max. "Birds are singing. Flowers are about to bloom. It's time to get out of bed."

"I *know* it is spring," said Maggie. "I know the birds are singing, and I know the flowers are about to bloom. What I do *not* know is what that has to do with me getting out of bed."

"*I've* been up for hours," said Max. "Spring is a busy time. So let's get busy with spring cleaning."

"Spring may be a busy time for you," said
Maggie. "For me, it is a time for doing nothing."
And she pulled the blanket over her head.

"My poor friend," said Max. "You must not feel
well. That's why you're still in bed."

Maggie groaned. "Max," she said, "I'm not sick. I just don't feel like doing anything. You may join me, if you like."

"Oh," said Max. "All right."

He sat in a rocking chair and tried to do nothing. But soon his foot forgot how to do nothing. It began to tap. The chair began to rock. And Max began to whistle.

Maggie opened one eye. "Okay," she said. "Tell me. What *is* spring cleaning?"

"I'm glad you asked," said Max. "During spring cleaning we brush away the cobwebs of winter. It is a time to scrub and polish. We'll make your little house as fresh and clean as spring itself!"

Maggie looked around the room. "It *is* a little dusty in here," she said.

"Yes," said Max. "So let's clean it. I will clean the bedroom, while you clean the kitchen."

Maggie got out of bed. She went to the closet. She got out a mop, a pail, a broom, and a dust cloth. Then she went to the kitchen. Maggie scrubbed the floor and ceiling. She washed the windows, pots, and pans until they sparkled.

With a satisfied smile, Maggie looked around her. "Max," she called, "come and see the kitchen!"

But Max did not answer. Maggie looked in the bedroom. There was Max, fast asleep in the rocking chair.

"Well," Maggie said, "it looks like Max and I were both right about spring. Spring is a good time for cleaning and working hard. But spring is also a good time for doing nothing at all."

Then Maggie climbed back into bed and fell sound asleep.

APRIL SHOWERS

One day in spring, Maggie went to visit Max. In her hands, she carried something wrapped in paper.

Maggie knocked on Max's door. No one answered. From inside, Maggie heard loud singing and water running.

"I guess Max is in the shower," said Maggie.
"I'll let myself in." She opened the door.

"Max?" called Maggie. "Are you in the shower?"

"What?" said Max.

"Are you in the shower?" said Maggie, in a
louder voice.

"I can't hear you," called Max. "I'm in the shower!"

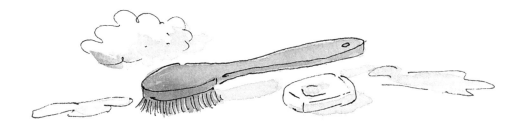

Maggie sat down to wait. Soon the singing stopped and so did the water. Max came out smiling.

"There!" said Max. "Now I'm ready."

"Ready for what?" asked Maggie.

"The flowers," said Max.

"What flowers?" said Maggie.

"I heard that April showers bring May flowers," said Max. "Today is the last day of April, so I took an extra long shower. Tomorrow is the first day of May. I bet I'll get a lot of flowers."

"Max," said Maggie, "I don't think that's what is meant by 'April showers bring May flowers.'"

"What does it mean then?" asked Max.

"It's just a saying. It means that the rain showers of April will help the flowers to grow in May," said Maggie.

"You mean the shower I took won't bring May flowers?" said Max.

"That's right," said Maggie. "To grow flowers you need to plant seeds first. Remember when I planted seeds in my garden at the beginning of April? The rain helped the seeds to grow."

"But *I* didn't plant any seeds," said Max sadly.
A small tear appeared in his eye. "I won't have
any flowers this spring."

"That's not true," said Maggie. She handed him the package wrapped in paper.

Max opened it and smiled. Inside was a beautiful bunch of flowers from Maggie's garden.

"Here are your May flowers—one day early,"
said Maggie. "Happy spring, Max!"

"Thank you!" said Max. "And happy spring to
you, too!"